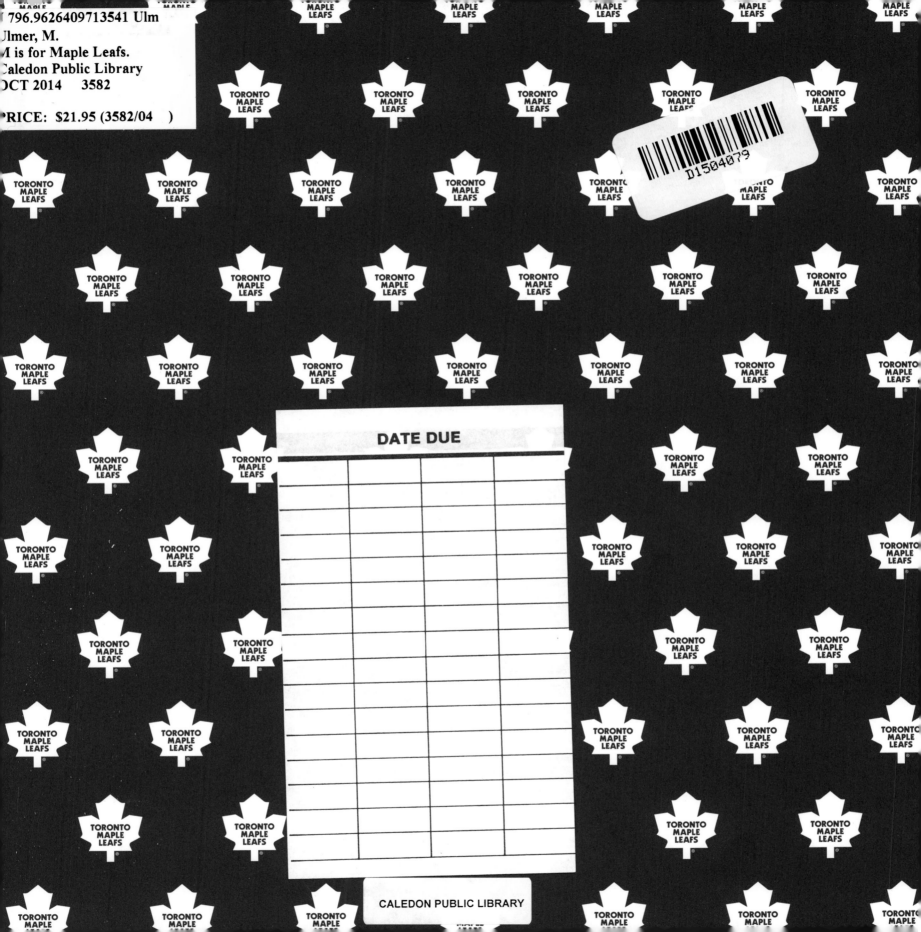

M IS FOR MAPLE LEAFS

An Official Toronto Maple Leafs Alphabet Book

Mike Ulmer *Illustrated by* Melanie Rose

FENN
TUNDRA

A is for Air Canada Centre,
the home of the Leafs,
where the thrills are divided
among 20,000 seats,
where the nights are electric,
where players find fame.
Toronto's the centre
of our national game.

Aa

Toronto's Air Canada Centre has been home to the Leafs since 1999.
The Leafs have played in three arenas: the Arena Gardens, Maple
Leaf Gardens, and Air Canada Centre.

Bb

B is the blue in the Blue and White.
They are colours all Maple Leafs bear.
For the white of the snow and the blue of the sky
are the only colours Leafs fans will wear.

The Leafs were known as the St. Pats in 1927.
Conn Smythe changed the uniforms from green
and white to blue and white to reflect the colours
of his old school, the University of Toronto.

Cc

It's a symbol, a C,
a letter on the chest.
But beneath it lies the giant heart
that beats inside the best.

C stands for captains and Maple Leafs
captains have come from all over, including
Kingston, Ontario (Doug Gilmour);
Bromma, Sweden (Mats Sundin); and
Edmonton, Alberta (Dion Phaneuf).

Dd

D is for dressing room,
where the centre of all
is the blue and white logo
surrounded by stalls.
It's uncovered on game days,
and while on the floor,
no skate can touch it
on the way out the door.

The Maple Leafs cover their team logo with a carpet, except during games.
Like many teams, the Leafs honour their logo by not stepping on it.

There are helmets, pads, gloves, and a whole room full of skates. Leafs players need the right equipment to prevent cuts and breaks.

Ee

The Leafs' equipment manager stocks an entire room full of every piece of equipment a player needs. Leafs players usually go through three or four pairs of skates per season.

Ff

Put the players where they belong
and drop the puck on the spot.
Now you know just how things start:
play begins on the faceoff dot.

When an official drops the puck between players from each team
to begin play, it's called a faceoff. The puck is put in play in the
red circle, or faceoff dot. It's important to win faceoffs because
it gives the team a head start in attacking or defending.

Gg

He slides, he stretches, he dives headlong;
he reasons, he guesses, he bets
to stop every puck that comes his way.
He's the goalie in the Maple Leafs' net.

The word "goalie" is short for goaltender. Unlike
forwards and defencemen, who have more than one job
when on the ice, the goalie's only job is to stop pucks.

Skip the line—just walk right through.
Step right up, they're expecting you.
It's where you go when you can get no better.
They'll ask for your stick and for your sweater.
If you're a player at the top of the game,
then you belong in the Hall of Fame.

Hh

For players, being a member of the Hockey Hall of Fame is a great honour. The Hall is located in Toronto, just a block north of Air Canada Centre, where the Hockey Hall of Fame Game is played each year.

Ii

To get the ice from flowing water,
to turn a pond into a rink,
takes lots of good equipment
and more math than you might think.

It takes 45,000 litres of water to make an NHL ice surface. That's enough water to fill 225 bathtubs! NHL ice is about 2 centimetres thick, or about the width of a puck.

They used to joke that when he began,
dinosaurs were hunting man.
J is for Johnny, the China Wall,
one of the greatest Leafs goalies of all.

Jj

Johnny Bower got his nickname, "the China Wall," because shooting against him was like shooting against a wall as thick and high as the Great Wall of China. Bower came to the Maple Leafs in 1958, at the age of 34. Most players are retired by that age, but Bower played an amazing 11 more full seasons for the Maple Leafs.

They were just kids, these dashing three—
Primeau, Conacher, and Jackson—
but the Kid Line was always guaranteed
to be the centre of the action.
With speed and dash and daring too,
they raided the opposing net.
They were just kids, but kids like these
are impossible to forget.

Kk

In the 1930s, "Gentleman" Joe Primeau, Charlie "Big Bomber" Conacher, and Harvey "Busher" Jackson were members of the Leafs' Kid Line—so named because all three players were very young. A line is composed of a centre and two wingers, one on each side.

Are you watching? Keep an eye.
It's almost time to change the lines.
Pay attention, be aware
of when to change a defensive pair.
Give a shout, rattle the gate.
That's the signal—don't be late.
There's no reason to drag your feet.
Skate like heck then take your seat.

L1

L is for line change. Though NHL players are in great physical condition, they still take shifts on the ice to give themselves time to recover. Changing "on the fly" means a team substitutes one, several, or all of the players on the ice while the play continues.

M is for the maple leaf.
It's a symbol we're happy to share
with the flag that waves across the land
and the sweater our Maple Leafs wear.

Mm

When Conn Smythe acquired the Maple Leafs, he wanted an emblem that represented Canada to adorn the team uniforms. He quickly settled upon the maple leaf because it was worn with pride by Canadian soldiers in the First World War.

N is for the numbers of the great 18,
the best of the best of the best.
Those magical numbers and magical games
gave us moments we'll never forget.
There's Ace and King and Turk and Hap,
don't forget the great China Wall too.
There's Mats Sundin and Leonard "Red" Kelly
and Tim Horton, to mention a few.

Nn

The Maple Leafs have recognized 18 of their best players by
honouring their numbers on banners hung above the ice.
Two numbers—the 6 worn by Ace Bailey and the 5 worn
by Bill Barilko—are retired and will never be worn again.

I know it's very hard to believe
that six clubs once made the league.
In the long ago days of the Original Six,
every player knew each other's tricks.

Oo

The Leafs used to play in a six-team NHL. The National Hockey
League has grown by five times since then, but until 1967 the
Toronto Maple Leafs, the Detroit Red Wings, the Montreal
Canadiens, the New York Rangers, the Boston Bruins, and the
Chicago Blackhawks were the only teams in the league.

Pp

They strive and lunge and dive to get it.
They'll chase and lean—and crunch.
But with a whistle they'll forget it,
as if it didn't matter much.
To be a puck would not be easy,
a fate to be deplored;
to sometimes be the goal of players,
and other times be ignored.

Pucks are made of hard rubber and weigh
160 grams. Because players can shoot pucks
as fast as 175 kilometres per hour, protective
netting behind the nets keeps spectators safe.

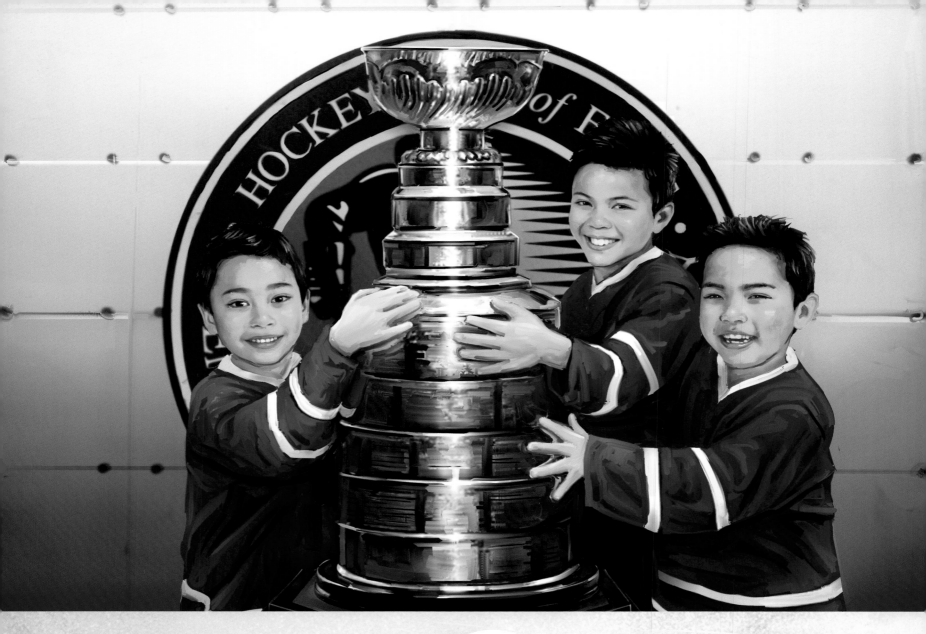

Every season starts with Q:
it represents the yearly quest.
To end the season by embracing
the trophy for the very best.

Qq

The Stanley Cup® is the most famous trophy in North American sports. Each team begins every new season on a quest for the Cup, but only one of the league's 30 teams will take it home.

You always have to check in last.
Your locker's not in the nicest space.
You're at the end when the tape is passed.
You always have to know your place.
But there's nowhere you would rather stay
to take in every sight and smell.
And there's nowhere you would rather play
when you're a rookie in the NHL.

Rr

For rookies, making the NHL means the chance to play alongside and against players they consider heroes. As a sign of respect, NHL rookies often take their turn after older players in the lineup for food and to board the team airplane.

1917
Great Uncle
Charlie
& Friends

Miller Farm

Conner &
Tim
2014

One hundred winters, one hundred springs.
Hundreds of centres, thousands of wings.
One hundred falls, one hundred starts.
Countless fans with Maple Leaf hearts.
One hundred years, one hundred seasons.
We love the Leafs for millions of reasons.

Ss

The Maple Leafs celebrate their 100th birthday on
December 19, 2017. One of the NHL's Original Six teams,
the Leafs have thrilled countless fans around the world.

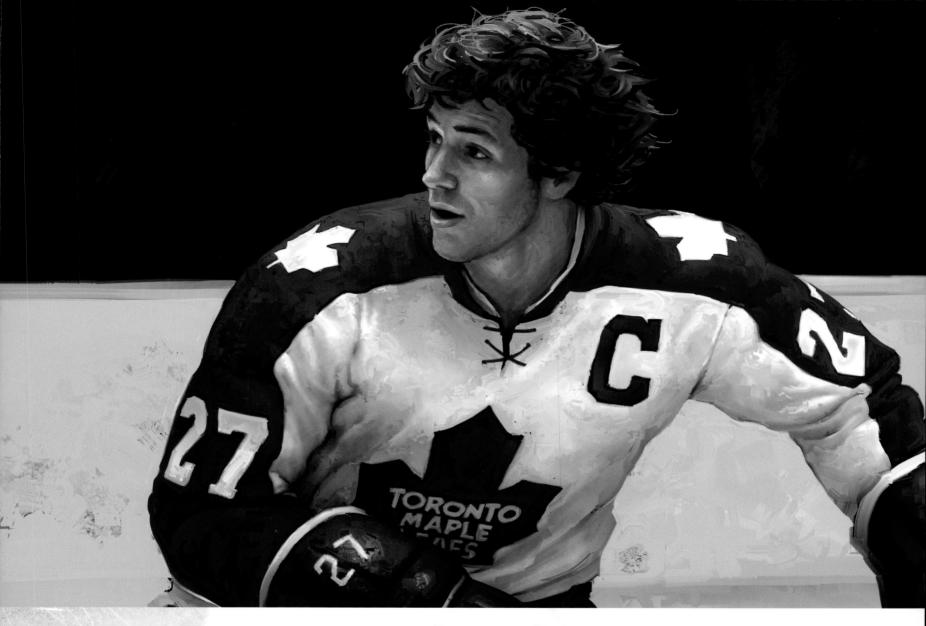

There's never been a ten-point game,
with one particular exception:
when Darryl Sittler's ten-point night
led to the Bruins' dejection.
Six goals and four assists
would be a stunning week.
But to get ten points in just one night?
Now that's a scoring streak!

Tt

In 1976, Darryl Sittler set a new NHL record for most points in a game when he scored ten points—six goals and four assists—in an 11-4 win over Boston. The Bruins goalie that night, Dave Reece, never played another NHL game.

It's just around the corner
from the home of the Maple Leafs.
You needn't even bother
to cross a crowded street.
So take the train to a Maple Leafs game,
all you in Maple Leafs Nation.
Don't forget! Don't miss your stop!
Get off at Union Station.

Uu

Fans heading to a Maple Leafs game get off at Union Station, which is connected to Air Canada Centre. Union is one of 69 stations that make up the Toronto Transit Commission (TTC) subway system.

V is for the Vezina Trophy.
It's what they give the very best,
who turn away the enemy shooters
and dazzle with their play in net.

Vv

Each year, the top goalie in the NHL is awarded the Vezina Trophy.
Five Maple Leafs goalies—Turk Broda, Johnny Bower, Terry
Sawchuk, Al Rollins, and Harry Lumley—have won the Vezina.

It's not as if there is a shortage
of Bobs or Teds or Ricks or Petes,
who at one time or another
have skated for the Maple Leafs.
But when counting all the Wendels,
the job is quickly done.
There is no list that could be shorter
than a list that numbers one.

Ww

Wendel Clark, who played for the team during the 1980s and '90s, is one of the Leafs' most popular players. To this day, whenever they see Wendel, Leafs fans burst into applause.

It's where you always want to be
if you have scoring on your mind.
It is the very best location
for bagging goals that you will find.
So if you want to hit the score sheet,
X will mark the spot.
Hang your hat where the gunners go,
make your way right to the slot.

The area just in front of the net is called the slot. It is considered a great location for goal scorers because they are close to the net and can aim for any spot.

Your inside voice is perfectly fine
for quiet talks and reading time.
Whispering and voices light
are what you want when the time is night.
But when darkness comes and the Leafs are on,
they need your cheering, loud and strong.
So yell and shout and scream and roar
each time your favourites raise the score.

Yy

Y is for yell. When the Leafs score, fans from all
across the land let loose with a yell.

I think that I will never see
a shy and quiet referee.
They often get a night of blame
and have yet to play just one home game.
Players with a beef or gripe
turn to the zebra, wearing stripes.

Zz

"Zebra" is a nickname given to NHL referees or linesmen since both the animal and the NHL official wear stripes. The distinctive uniforms make them easy to spot as they zip around the ice.

A is also for **assist**. An assist is given to one or two teammates who touch the puck in the moments just before a goal is scored.

B is also for **backcheck**. A forward who returns to his own zone to prevent a good scoring chance is known as a backchecker.

C is also for **Carlton the Bear**. The Leafs' friendly mascot is named after Carlton Street in Toronto. The Leafs' old home, Maple Leaf Gardens, was located at 60 Carlton Street, which is why Carlton wears the number 60 on his jersey.

D is also for **defence**. Because they don't skate as much as forwards, defencemen usually play more during a game. Defencemen work in pairs and often play with the same partners for months, even years.

E is also for **eleven**. The maple leaf in the team logo has eleven points.

F is also for **fans**. During the playoffs, fans pack Maple Leafs Square behind Air Canada Centre to watch the Leafs on the giant screen.

G is also for Maple Leaf **Gardens**. The Gardens was built in 1931 and was the home of the Leafs for 68 years.

H is also for **home ice**. Players often talk about home ice advantage. The support of the home fans can have an impact on the game, as can the home team's right to make the final substitution of the game. Is it any wonder most teams play better at home than on the road?

I is also for **icing**. If a player shoots the puck from his side of centre ice and the puck crosses the opposing team's goal line without being touched, he is called for icing. The whistle blows, a faceoff is held in that player's end, and his team is not allowed to substitute players.

J is also for **jump**. In hockey, jump is a noun, not a verb. When a hockey team has jump, it means they are playing with energy and effort.

K is also for **Kennedy**. A player with great courage and determination, Ted Kennedy won five Stanley Cups with the Leafs during the 1940s and '50s.

L is also for **Leonard** "Red" Kelly. Red Kelly came to the Maple Leafs in the middle of the 1958–59 season and won four Stanley Cups with Toronto.

M is also for **major** and **minor** penalties. A team that is penalized must play a man short. A minor penalty such as hooking or tripping lasts for two minutes or until the team with the man advantage, or power play, has scored. A major penalty such as hitting from behind lasts five minutes.

N is also for **neutral** zone. The neutral zone is the area between the two blue lines. A red centre line divides the neutral zone in half.

O is also for **offside**. A player is offside when the puck is passed from behind one blue line to the far side of the other blue line, or when a player touches the puck after preceding it into the offensive zone.

P is also for **pulling** the goalie. When a team is down by a goal or two late in the game, they often remove their goalie and put another forward on the ice. This gives the team a better chance of scoring.

Q is also for Pat **Quinn**. Quinn was born in Hamilton, Ontario, near Toronto, and played defence for the team in the 1960s. From 1998–2006, he was the team's head coach.

R is also for **rebound**. When a shot hits the goalie and stays in play, it is known as a rebound.

S is also for Mats **Sundin**. Mats scored more goals and recorded more points than any other Maple Leaf. The great Swede captained the Maple Leafs for ten seasons, from 1997 to 2008.

T is also for **Toronto**. Leafs fans are so enthusiastic about their team that Toronto has often been called the centre of the hockey universe.

U is also for **underdog**. An underdog is a player or team that is not expected to win. One of the great things about sports is that with effort an underdog can beat the odds.

V is also for **victory**. The Leafs record for victories or wins in an 82-game season is 45. Victories count for two points in the standings, so when a player says, "We got the two points," it means his team won the game.

W is also for **whiskers**. Over the years, a few Leafs players—like Wendel Clark and Lanny McDonald—wore whiskers all the time. Many players grow more facial hair during the playoffs for luck.

X is also for Xs and Os. Coaches use Xs and Os on boards or video screens to plan plays and show players where to go.

Y is also for **Yushkevich**. During the 1990s and early 2000s, defenceman Dmitry Yushkevich and his friend Danny Markov, both from Russia, were one of the Leafs' better defence pairs.

Z is also for **Zamboni**® Machine. The Zamboni® was invented in 1949 by Frank Zamboni, a California man who owned a rink and needed a machine that could clean and scrape the ice and apply a fresh coat of water.

Published in Canada by Fenn/Tundra, a division of Random House of Canada Limited,
One Toronto Street, Suite 300, Toronto, Ontario M5C 2V6

Published in the United States by Random House of Canada Limited,
P.O. Box 1030, Plattsburgh, New York 12901

Library of Congress Control Number: 2014934596

Library and Archives Canada Cataloguing in Publication

Ulmer, Michael, 1959-, author
M Is for Maple Leafs / by Michael Ulmer ; illustrated by Melanie Rose.

ISBN 978-1-77049-798-6 (bound).—ISBN 978-1-77049-799-3 (pbk.)

1. English language—Alphabet—Juvenile literature. 2. Alphabet books.
3. Toronto Maple Leafs (Hockey team)—Juvenile literature.
4. Hockey—Juvenile literature.
I. Rose, Melanie, illustrator II. Title.

PE1155.U46 2014   j421'.1   C2014-901472-4

Edited by Harry Endrulat and Elizabeth Kribs
Designed by Jennifer Lum
The text was set in Twentieth Century and Minion
www.randomhouse.ca

Printed and bound in Canada

1 2 3 4 5 6   19 18 17 16 15 14